GORP

TOPO
MAP

TRAIL
MAP

Dedicated to
Finn, Brynn, and Morgan
and
to young hikers everywhere

Special thanks to
Jenny Tilson
and
Scott Kloos

Library of Congress Cataloging-in-Publication Data available.

ISBN 978-1-4521-7461-7

Manufactured in China.

Design by Ryan Hayes.
Typeset in Sentinel.
The illustrations in this book were rendered in gouache, ink, and pencil.

10 9 8 7 6 5

Chronicle Books LLC
680 Second Street
San Francisco, California 94107

Chronicle Books—we see things differently. Become part of our community at www.chroniclekids.com.

THE HIKE

ALISON FARRELL

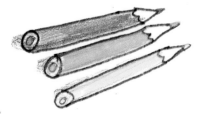

chronicle books·san francisco

mountain
chickadee

We are going on a hike.

Wren   El   Hattie   Bean

It's our favorite thing to do.

knot hole

barred owlets

salmonberry

deer fern

English ivy

old-man's beard
swarm of bees
HEY WAIT FOR MEEEEE!
burdock
wild columbine
chipmunk nest
taproot

In the beginning, we run like maniacs.

Until a ripe patch of thimbleberries
slows us down.

Douglas fir bough

western
toad

El teaches us how to make leaf baskets.

The hike gets steep
and the trail narrows.

porcupine climbing
a cedar tree

hollow
tree

vanilla leaf

orb weaver spider

A deer walks past.
Bean sneezes.

black
morel
mushroom

salal

The deer vanishes so quick, we wonder if it was ever really there.

raven

plunge
waterfall

horsetail

Soon, El is tired too.

At the top, Wren takes out her flag, El reads her poem, and Hattie releases feathers into the wind.

We did it.

Indian
paintbrush

Gemini

Auriga

Perseus

Pegasus

Orion

Taurus

Pleiades

COSMOS

Some things I saw today:

Steller's Jay

. Smart

. Noisy

. In the CORVIDAE family along with: crows, ravens, magpies, and jays

BARRED OWLETS

HATTIE SAYS BARRED OWLS SOUND LIKE:

Who cooks for you?

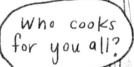

Who cooks for you all?

Psst... why does she keep asking? No one ever cooks for us!

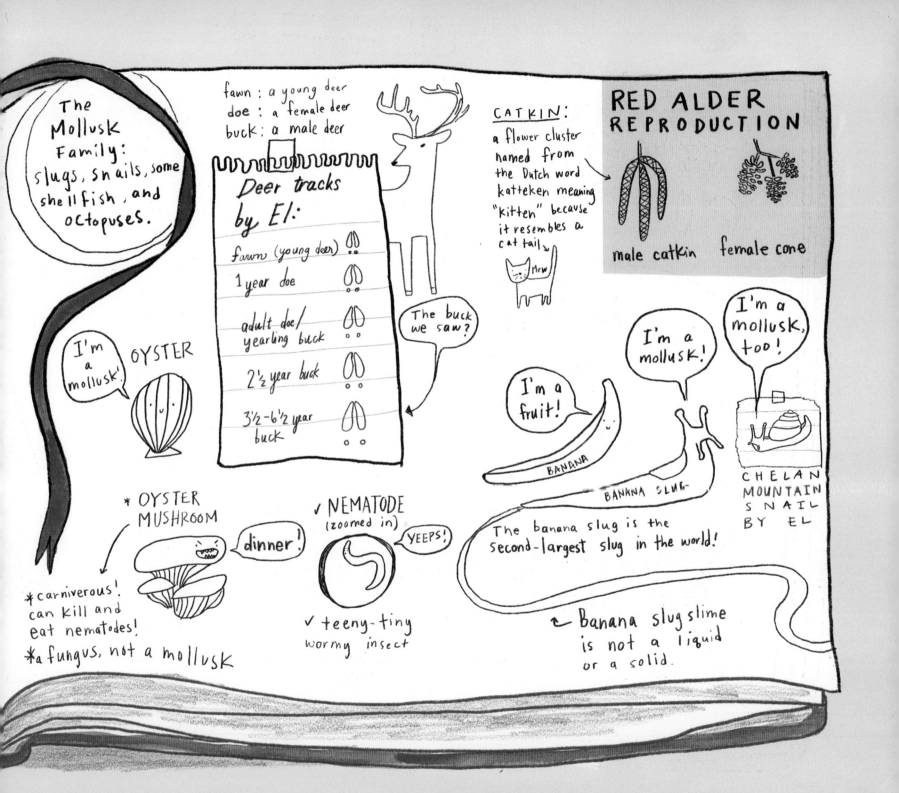

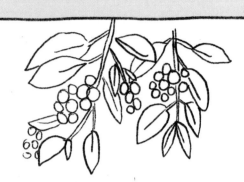

 snowberry aka GHOSTBERRY

 BOO

delicious for 🐦's
toxic for 👶's

Vanilla Leaf

insect repelling!

dry to make a delicious, vanilla-flavored tea!

Redwood Sorrel

tart!

edible   lemon-y

3 ♡-shaped leaves

horsetail

aka equisetum →

reproduces by spores not seeds!

I'm a living fossil!*

horsetail stems are so rough

they can scour cooking pots

*also alive in the Paleozoic Era
approximately 300 million years ago

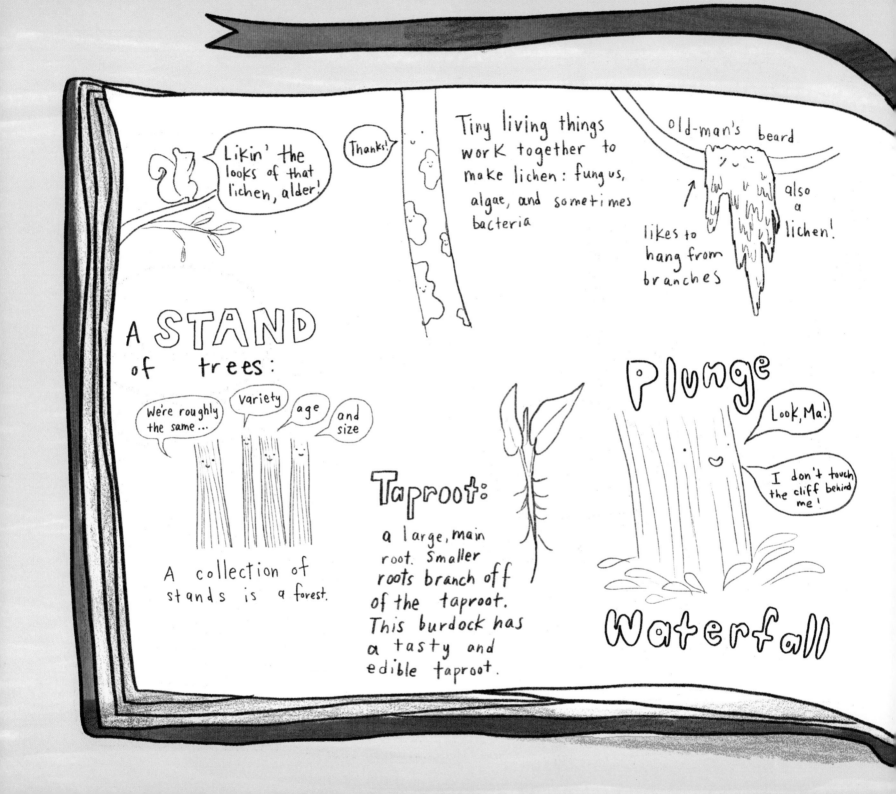

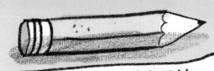